CPC

I Can Eat with Chopsticks

By Lin Xin

Copyright © 2018 by Shanghai Press and Publishing Development Co., Ltd.

This book is edited and designed by the Editorial Committee of *Cultural China* series

Story and Illustrations: Lin Xin
Translation: Yijin Wert

Editors: Wu Yuezhou, Anna Nguyen
Editorial Director: Zhang Yicong

Senior Consultants: Sun Yong, Wu Ying, Yang Xinci
Managing Director and Publisher: Wang Youbu

ISBN: 978-1-60220-452-2

Address any comments about *I Can Eat with Chopsticks* to:

Better Link Press
99 Park Ave
New York, NY 10016
USA

or

Shanghai Press and Publishing Development Co., Ltd.
F 7 Donghu Road, Shanghai, China (200031)
Email: comments_betterlinkpress@hotmail.com

Printed in China by Shenzhen Donnelley Printing Co., Ltd.

1 3 5 7 9 10 8 6 4 2

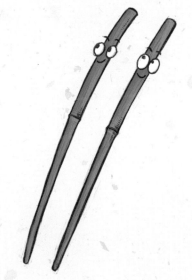

A Story in English and Chinese

I Can Eat with Chopsticks

By Lin Xin

The Tale of the Chopstick Brothers and How They Became A Pair

筷子

Better Link Press

On a drizzling spring morning, Dad took his daughter Little Mo to the bamboo forest. While he was digging out bamboo, Little Mo picked up a small bamboo stick to play.

春雨滴答，爸爸带着女儿小默来到竹林，他挖竹笋，小默捡竹枝玩。

After returning home, Little Mo enjoyed lunch with her mom and dad around the table.

回到家,爸爸妈妈和小默开开心心地围在一起吃午饭。

Dad laid a pot of extremely hot soup on the table. Little Mo and Mom wondered what the easiest way would be to get the vegetables out of the soup.

爸爸端上一锅汤，好烫！怎么才能捞出汤里的蔬菜呢？妈妈和小默都犯了难。

"I can help!" said the Little Bamboo Stick. Flinging himself from Little Mo's sack, he jumped into the pot and began picking out the vegetables.

小竹枝从小默的袋子里蹦出来，说道："我能帮上忙。"它跳进汤碗，挑起蔬菜。

The family were all surprised.

When Little Mo was about to finish the rice in her bowl, the Little Bamboo Stick jumped into her bowl and gathered all the remains for her.

全家人都惊呆了。

待小默快吃完饭时，小竹枝跳进碗里，将剩下的米粒拢在一起。

During the next few days, the Little Bamboo Stick helped out a lot in the kitchen. When Dad was making the egg drop soup, the Little Bamboo Stick jumped into the bowl to stir the eggs. Soon the eggs were mixed evenly in the soup.

随后几天，小竹枝在厨房里玩得好开心。爸爸做蛋羹时，小竹枝跳进碗里不停地转圈，一会儿汤和蛋就搅匀了。

When Mom was making steamed bread, the Little Bamboo Stick quickly kneaded the dough. The steamed bread was made in no time.

妈妈做馒头时，小竹枝在面团上手舞足蹈。一会儿，馒头就做好了。

One day, Mom made a bowl of noodles. The Little Bamboo Stick sprung into action as usual, but he could not pick up the noodles. This made him very upset.

一天，妈妈端来一碗面条。小竹枝兴冲冲地跳进碗里，可是他怎么也捞不起面条。小竹枝不高兴了。

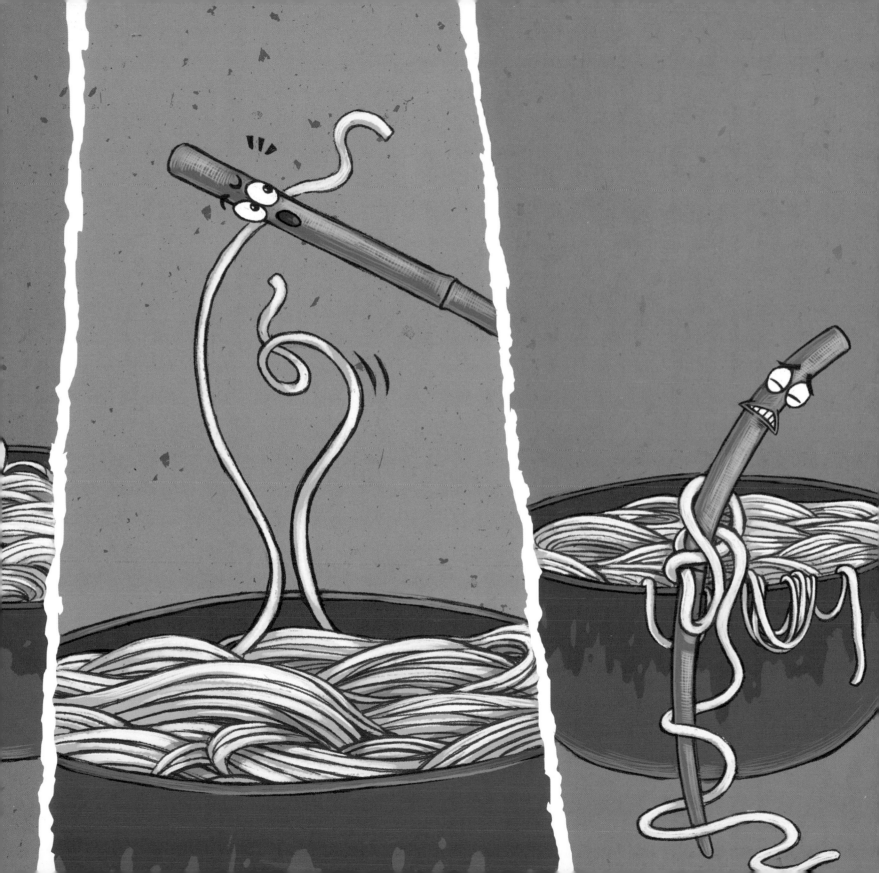

"What's wrong?" asked Little Mo.

"I could not help Mom to pick up the noodles. I don't think I can do it alone," said the Little Bamboo Stick.

"Don't worry! I will find you a friend!" said Little Mo.

"小竹枝, 你怎么啦? "小默问道。

"我没能帮妈妈捞起面条, 也许单靠我一个人还不行。"小竹枝说。

"别担心! 我给你找一个帮手吧。"小默说。

Little Mo and the Little Bamboo Stick went back to the bamboo forest and found a similar sized bamboo stick to bring home.

小默与小竹枝又回到那片竹林，找到另一根差不多的小竹枝，带回了家。

Little Mo had the two bamboo sticks in her hands, but she couldn't figure out how they could pick up the noodles. The bamboo sticks didn't know what to do either.

She practiced with the two bamboo sticks every day trying to find the answer.

小默抓着两根小竹枝，可仍然不知道怎么捞起面条。小竹枝也不知所措。

小默和两根小竹枝天天练习，天天琢磨。

Finally one day, Little Mo put two sticks together like a kitchen tong and picked up the noodles.

She was thrilled to figure out how to use them.

终于有一天，小默使得两根小竹枝像夹子一样，夹起了面条。

找到办法的小默高兴极了。

The next morning, Little Mo split a bun with the two bamboo sticks and shared the other half with Mom.

第二天早饭时，小默用两根小竹枝扒开一只包子，分了一半给妈妈。

At lunch, Little Mo was able to pick up green vegetable leaves with the two bamboo sticks.

午饭时, 小默用两根小竹枝夹起青菜叶子。

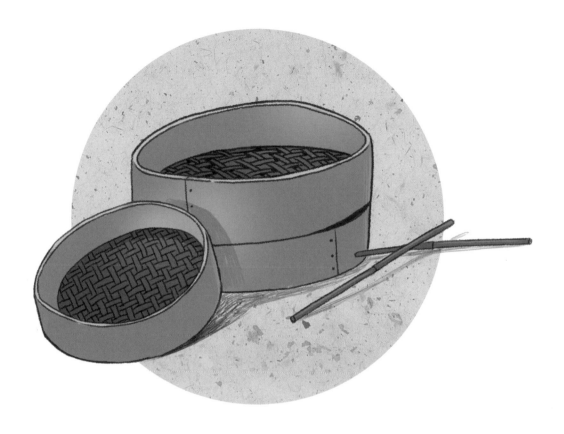

At dinner, Little Mo was able to pick up a little pork dumpling with the bamboo sticks and easily put it into her mouth.

晚饭时，小默用两根小竹枝提起小笼包，毫不费力地送到嘴边。

"The two of us can help you pick up noodles and vegetables, stir eggs and split pork buns," said the pair of Little Bamboo Sticks with pride.

"Then why don't we call you two chopsticks!" said Dad.

"捞面、挑蔬菜、打蛋、分包子，我们兄弟都可以帮上忙。"小竹枝自豪地说。

"那就叫你们筷子吧。"爸爸说。

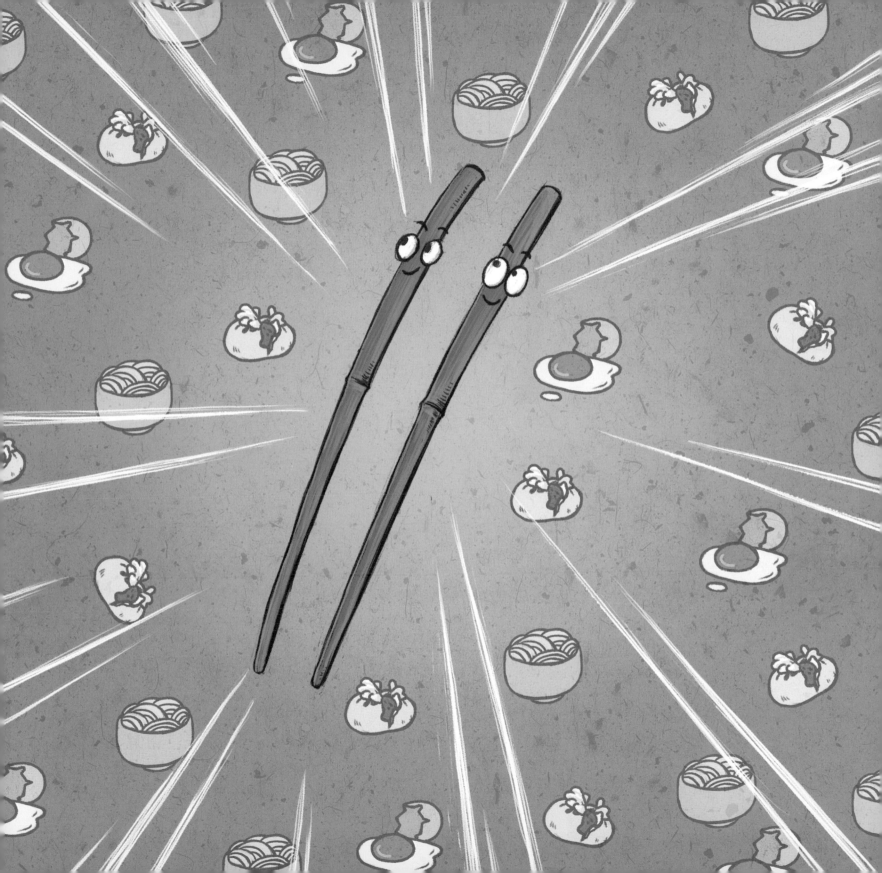

Suddenly, the two excited chopstick brothers accidentally rolled off the table .

突然，兴奋的筷子兄弟不小心从桌上滚到了地下。

Dad immediately thought of a way to prevent this from happening again. He shaped one end of the stick from point to square.

"We don't need to worry about rolling off the table anymore!" the chopstick brothers said happily.

爸爸急中生智，将筷子两兄弟的一头磨成方形。

"我们再也不用担心滚下桌子啦！"筷子兄弟开心地说道。

The Right Way for Holding and Using Chopsticks
筷子的正确使用方法

Hold the chopsticks with your thumb, index finger and middle finger comfortably.

用拇指、食指和中指轻轻拿住筷子。

The thumb is beside the index finger.

拇指要放在食指旁边。

Move the upper chopstick up and down with your index finger and middle finger.

用食指和中指移动上面的筷子。

The tips of the chopsticks should be lined up evenly.

筷子尖要对齐。

Place your hand roughly one-third the way down from the top of the chopsticks.

手放在距离筷子尾部1/3处。

Use your ring finger to support the chopsticks.

无名指垫在下边。

The lower chopstick should remain more or less stationary.

下面筷子固定。

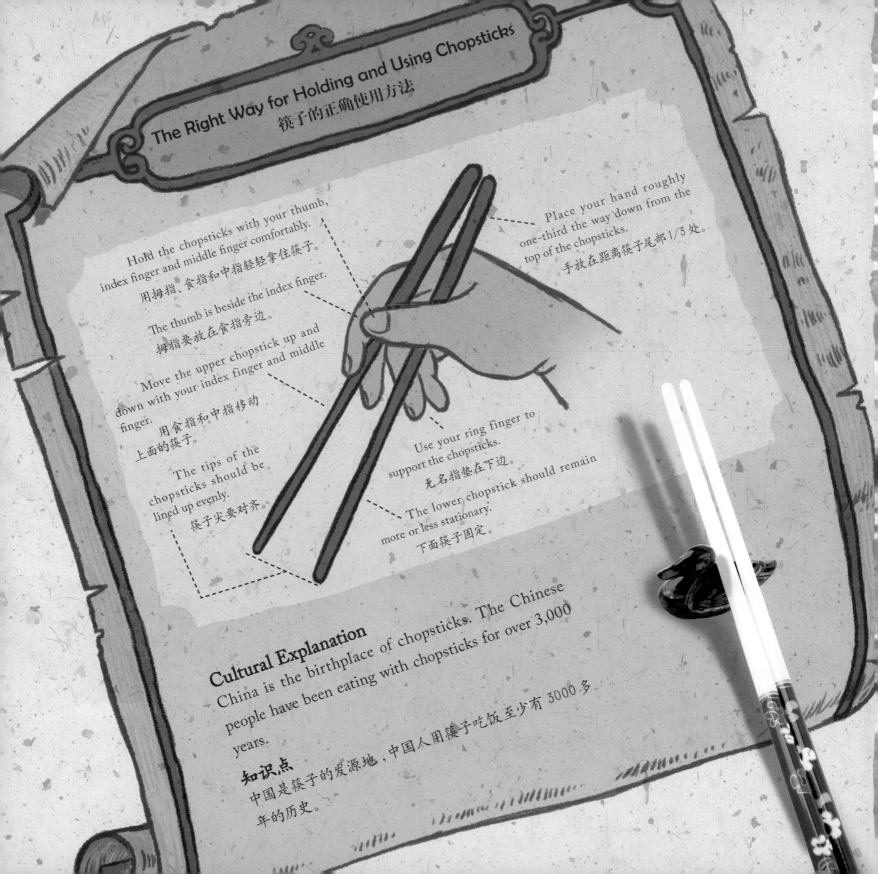

Cultural Explanation

China is the birthplace of chopsticks. The Chinese people have been eating with chopsticks for over 3,000 years.

知识点

中国是筷子的发源地，中国人用筷子吃饭至少有3000多年的历史。

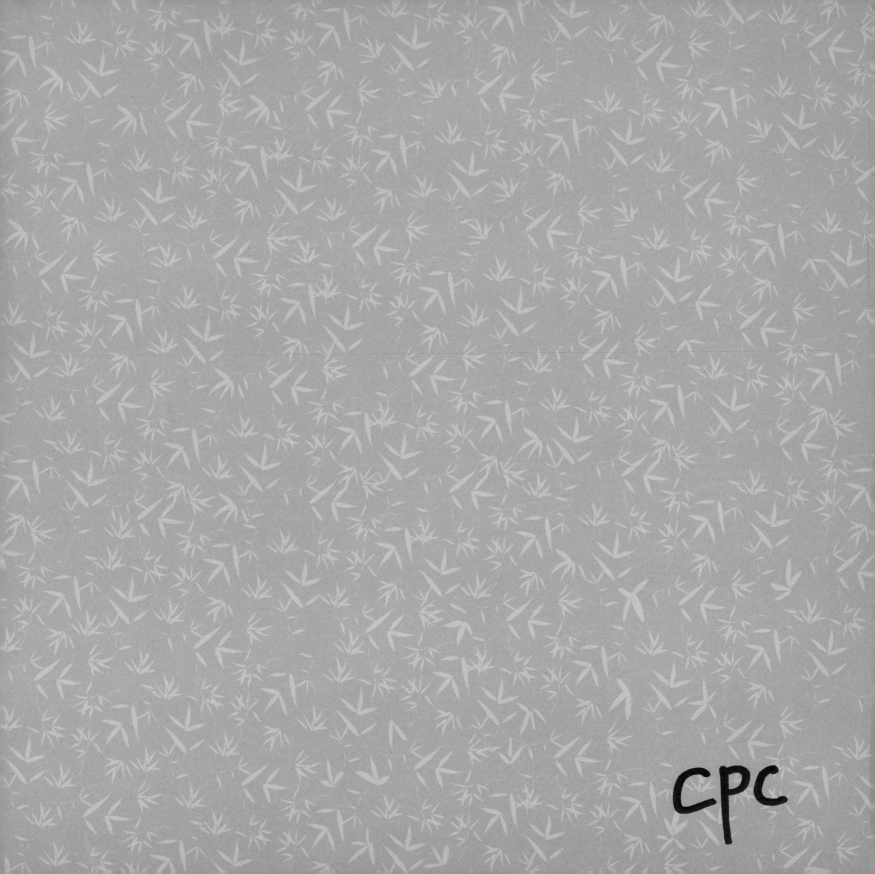